SHIRLEY TEMPLE BLACK
ACTRESS TO AMBASSADOR

The Women of Our Time® Series

SHIRLEY TEMPLE BLACK

ACTRESS TO AMBASSADOR

BY JAMES HASKINS
Illustrated by Donna Ruff

VIKING KESTREL

VIKING KESTREL
Published by the Penguin Group
Viking Penguin Inc., 40 West 23rd Street, New York, New York 10010, U.S.A.
Penguin Books Ltd, 27 Wrights Lane, London W8 5TZ England
Penguin Books Australia Ltd, Ringwood, Victoria, Australia
Penguin Books Canada Ltd, 2801 John Street, Markham, Ontario, Canada L3R 1B4
Penguin Books (N.Z.) Ltd, 182–190 Wairau Road, Auckland 10, New Zealand

Penguin Books Ltd, Registered Offices: Harmondsworth, Middlesex, England

First published in 1988 by Viking Penguin Inc.
Published simultaneously in Canada
Text copyright © James Haskins, 1988
Illustrations copyright © Donna Ruff, 1988
All rights reserved
Women of Our Time® is a registered trademark of Viking Penguin Inc.
LIBRARY OF CONGRESS CATALOGING IN PUBLICATION DATA
Haskins, James, Shirley Temple Black/by James Haskins; illustrated by Donna Ruff.
p. cm.—(Women of our time)
Summary: A biography of the child actress who was known as "America's Sweetheart"
and who, as an adult, became active in politics and served as the first
woman Chief of Protocol at the White House.
ISBN 0-670-81957-3
1. Temple, Shirley, 1928– —Juvenile literature. 2. Motion
picture actors and actresses—United States—Biography—Juvenile
literature. [1. Temple, Shirley, 1928– . 2. Actors and
actresses.] I. Ruff, Donna, ill. II. Title. III. Series
PN2287.T33H3 1988 791.43′028′0924—dc19 [B] [92] 87-34076

Printed in the United States of America
by Haddon Craftsmen, Bloomsburg, Pennsylvania
Set in Garamond #3
1 2 3 4 5 92 91 90 89 88

CONTENTS

1

Birth of a Star

The time was 1934. All across America, people were out of work and out of hope. In Hollywood, moviemakers were trying hard to cheer up the country. The Fox Film company came up with the idea for a film called *Stand Up and Cheer*. It was about an imaginary government department called the Department of Amusement. The job of the Secretary of Amusement was to send teams of performers around the country to bring smiles to the people and make them forget their troubles.

Toward the end, an entertainer named Dugan (played

by James Dunn) sang a song called "Baby, Take a Bow." While he was singing, a little child came through his legs and sang the words, "Daddy, take a bow."

She wore a polka-dot dress with so many petticoats underneath that the skirt stuck straight out. She had golden hair in ringlets and two dimples as big as the polka-dots on her dress. And when she laughed she seemed to light up the movie screen. She was five-year-old Shirley Temple, and she was about to become the biggest star in Hollywood. For the next seven years, she was "America's Sweetheart." Her picture was on magazine covers. People bought thousands of Shirley Temple dolls and paper dolls. Mothers named their newborn daughters Shirley after her. Little girls, and their mothers, tried to create hairdos with Shirley Temple ringlets. When she caught a cold, she made headlines.

Looking back, grown-up Shirley Temple tries to remember what it was like to be a little girl and a big star. Many years have passed since then. Today, Shirley Temple Black is a grandmother. She has also been a member of the United States delegation to the United Nations, United States Ambassador to Ghana, and the first woman Chief of Protocol at the White House in Washington, D.C.

But most people still remember her best as Little Shirley Temple, the curly-topped tot with a dimpled smile who captured the hearts of American movie-goers back in the 1930s.

They look at her and say things like, "I can't believe you're a grandmother." When she makes a speech at a big meeting of politicians, the orchestra is likely to play "On the Good Ship Lollipop," one of the songs she made famous when she was a tiny movie star.

Shirley Temple Black takes all this in stride. She knows she can never forget the child who was once the biggest star in Hollywood. In fact, she knows that it sometimes has helped her to have that kind of famous past. But she has managed to have a full and happy adult life too, and she hopes that people have come to respect her for the things she has done as a grown-up. She once said of her childhood and of Little Shirley Temple, "I think upon the me of those days as my little sister. I know her very well, but not as myself."

Shirley Jane Temple never had a real little sister. In fact, she was the only girl in her family. She was the third child born to George and Gertrude Temple. The first two were boys: John and George, Jr. Gertrude loved her sons, but she prayed for a girl.

In 1927, Gertrude Temple became pregnant again. John was twelve and George seven. This time Gertrude was certain the baby was going to be a girl. She also believed that if she played good music, looked at great paintings, and gazed at the beauties of nature during her pregnancy, her little girl would be talented and beautiful.

Sure enough, the baby born on April 23, 1928, was a girl, and Gertrude and George Temple were overjoyed. They placed her in a bassinet in the living room, right across from the battery-powered radio. Gertrude played classical music on the radio for the infant Shirley Jane. She also played popular recordings of songs like "Life Is Just a Bowl of Cherries." By the time Shirley was eight months old, she would stand up in her crib whenever she heard music. Her mother said that, when Shirley started to walk, "She walked on her toes. From the time she took her first step, she ran on her toes, as if she were dancing."

In the fall of 1929, when Shirley was a year-and-a-half old, the country went into a severe economic depression. Many people lost all their money, not to mention their hopes for better times. So many people tried to take out their savings that banks across the country had to close their doors.

George Temple was the manager of a branch bank in Santa Monica, California, where the Temples lived. His bank closed for a while, and he was laid off. Later, when it reopened, he got his job back, but at a much lower salary. Money was tight in the Temple household, but Gertrude Temple was not about to let go

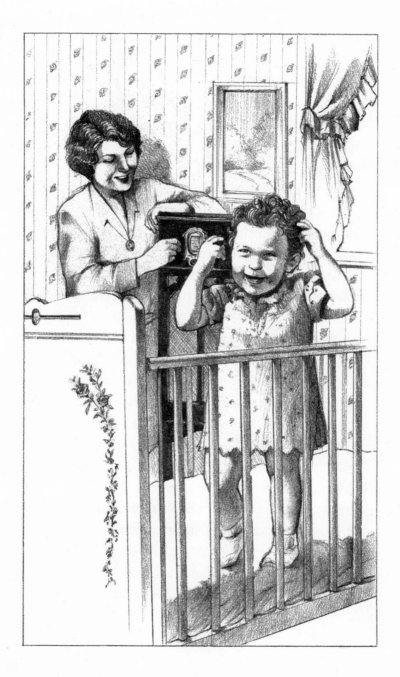

of her dream: little Shirley was going to have dancing lessons.

In the fall of 1931, when Shirley was three and a half, she enrolled at Meglin. At this school, children were taught all styles of dancing, as well as acting and singing. Many young Meglin students went on to movie careers.

One day, a few months after Shirley began taking lessons at Meglin, a movie director named Charles Lamont came to the school. He wanted to see if he could use any of the children in his movies. Shirley hid under a piano and had to be coaxed out to talk with the strange man who had come to look over the children.

Still, there was something about her that Lamont liked, and later he phoned Gertrude and asked her to bring Shirley to the studios of Educational, a new film company that turned out inexpensive movies at the rate of about one a week.

Shirley was one of dozens of children who were invited to the studio just after New Year's Day, 1932. Charles Lamont and his assistant, Earle Hammons, were walking on the grounds of the studio watching the children and their parents as they waited to be called.

Hammons later said, "One little child caught my coat and pulled it a little bit and I looked down and saw the most beautiful little thing, and I picked her up in my arms and I said, 'What's your name?' She said, 'Shirley.' I said, 'What are you doing here?' 'I'm going to work for you,' she answered. So I told Charlie, 'You want to watch her. She knows what she wants.'"

Educational wanted to do a series of short films called "Baby Burlesks," which were takeoffs on hit movies. The parts played in the movies by grown-ups would be played by preschool children in grown-up clothes. The first, called *War Babies*, was based on a movie called *What Price Glory?* Shirley was not chosen for a part. A little girl named Audrey Leonard got the role of the leading lady. But then Audrey became ill, and the producer called for Shirley.

In her first film role, Shirley played a French girl. Two soldiers fall in love with her. She wore a blouse with one bare shoulder and a rose in her hair, and she looked adorable playing a grown-up.

Jack Hays, the producer of Baby Burlesks, liked Shirley so much that he signed an agreement with the Temples which gave him an option, or first chance, to employ her before any other film company could do so. Shirley acted in seven more films for Educational in the next year and a half.

In one, she played the sexy film star Marlene Dietrich in a tight, sequined gown. In another, she played

a pint-sized Jane to a tiny Tarzan. As in the grown-up Tarzan films, her Jane wore a very brief costume. Nowadays, these eight-to-ten-minute films would be considered in poor taste. In fact, small children would not be allowed to play such roles, or appear in such costumes.

These films would also be outlawed as too dangerous for child actors. Once, Shirley had to ride in a cart pulled by an ostrich that panicked and ran away with Shirley in the cart. In the Tarzan and Jane film, a group of "natives" runs after the hero and heroine. Tarzan and Jane escape by putting a wire across their path. The "natives" were played by a group of little black boys who not only did trip on the wire but also suffered cuts to their legs. They all burst out crying, and so did Shirley, who still shudders when she remembers the accident.

But in those days when talking pictures were still new, there were no stunt men and women. There were no groups in the movie industry to set standards of safety or good taste. Shirley's parents did not see anything wrong with what she was doing. Anyway, the forty dollars a week she earned for a four-day workweek at Educational was money that the family needed in those Depression years.

By the middle of 1933, however, there was not as much work for Shirley in the Baby Burlesks. At five years old, she was no longer a baby and did not look as funny and cute in grown-up costumes as younger little girls did. Jack Hays still held the option on her services, and Shirley's mother kept after him to find work for her. He managed to get her some small parts in movies at the larger studios, like Paramount.

Henry Hathaway, an assistant at Paramount, loved Shirley the minute he saw her and called her a "little doll." He immediately cast her in *To the Last Man*, a Western starring Randolph Scott, and soon learned that there was more to little Shirley than her cuteness. She was exceptionally bright and had an amazing vocabulary for a five-year-old. He recalled many years later that he once found her sitting on a low truck that was used for moving furniture. He asked her if anything was wrong, and she replied, "You know, the ventilation here isn't very good. Not that it's hot and sultry, it's just the ventilation." Hays wondered how she had learned to talk like that when she hadn't even been to school yet.

But the movie audiences did not fall in love with Shirley the way Hays had. Critics paid no attention to her. Gertrude Temple was beginning to think that Shirley's brief movie career was over. Both she and her husband were worrying about how they were going to make ends meet with George's bank in trouble and little money coming in.

A stroke of luck changed all that.

2

America's Sweetheart

One afternoon, Gertrude decided to take Shirley to see a movie. They went to a theater on Wilshire Boulevard in the Beverly Hills section of Los Angeles. While her mother was buying the tickets, Shirley wandered over to the wall where photographs of stars were displayed.

As she looked at the pictures, she began to hum to herself and do a little dance. A musical director named Jay Gorney just happened to be in the lobby of the theater, and he was charmed by the little girl with reddish-gold ringlets humming and dancing all

by herself. In a short time, he had invited Gertrude
Temple to bring Shirley to the studios of the Fox Film
company.

At the studio, Gorney lifted Shirley up on a piano
and told her he was going to teach her a song. Then
he had her tap dance to the song. He was so excited
he could hardly contain himself. He called the Fox
chief of production, Winfield Sheehan. Sheehan hired

her for a small part in *Stand Up and Cheer*.

In the movie, Shirley had a full orchestra behind her, and an audience of dozens of chorus girls in spangled tights. When the movie was released, she was a smash hit.

One movie reviewer wrote, "A charming and remarkably engaging baby of perhaps five years, this little Shirley Temple proves a winning and natural child, with genius qualities of personality." Some critics said that she "stole the picture." Winfield Sheehan wasted no time in offering the Temples a seven-year contract at $150 a week.

Once her parents signed the contract for Shirley with Fox Films, Shirley became "the property of" the studio. In those days, film studios had that kind of control over their stars. They could, for example, say whatever they wanted to in their "official biographies" of stars. It was customary to subtract years from the ages of female stars, and Shirley was no exception. Fox decided that if Shirley was cute and bright at five, she would seem even more so if she was four. So, Shirley's studio-produced biography listed her age as four. After a time, Shirley got so used to the idea of being a year younger than she really was that she believed it. Not until the celebration of her twelfth birthday did she find out that she was really thirteen.

The other thing a studio could do was to "loan" a star it had under contract to another film company. Fox Films did this with Shirley in the fall of 1934 when they loaned her to Paramount. Fox continued to pay Shirley $150 a week, but it charged Paramount $1000 for just a couple weeks' worth of Shirley's work on *Little Miss Marker*. In this way, Fox made money on Shirley—by having her appear in its own films and also by loaning her out to other studios.

By 1935, when she had been with Fox for just a year, Shirley was one of the top box-office draws in Hollywood. By 1938 she was number one, which means that more people went to the movies just to see her than to see any other star. She was "America's sweetheart."

People couldn't stop talking about her dimples, her bright eyes and curly hair. These became her trademarks, and three Fox films written especially for her were titled *Bright Eyes* (1934), *Curly Top* (1935), and *Dimples* (1936).

The Ideal Toy and Novelty Company in New York City brought out a Shirley Temple doll for the 1934 Christmas season, and thousands were sold. There were also paper dolls, coloring books, and records of Shirley singing songs she had made famous in movies, like "On the Good Ship Lollipop" from *Bright Eyes*.

Shirley got tons of fan mail, more than any adult star. On her "eighth" birthday (really her ninth) in 1937, she received 135,000 gifts from all over the world. By this time, she was a star worldwide, for her films were released in foreign countries as well as in the United States.

Reporters and photographers followed her almost everywhere she went. Her picture was on the cover of national magazines, and anyone who wanted to read the articles could find out what she liked to eat (ice cream sodas), her favorite colors (red and white), that she had sucked her thumb until she was two years old.

Shirley was so used to being interviewed that one time when she was talking with a reporter she pointed to a pile of magazines nearby and said, "I'll bet you a nickel that if you pick up any one of those magazines, my picture will be in it." The writer reached into the middle of the stack. Just as Shirley had said, there was a photograph of her in the magazine he chose.

It was the height of the Great Depression, and people desperately needed something to make them smile. Movies were only fifteen cents then, so many people could afford that. Little Shirley made them feel warm and happy. So did Rin Tin Tin, another big star of the 1930s. Many years later, Shirley Temple said, "People in the Depression wanted something to cheer them up, and they fell in love with a dog and a little girl."

Whatever the reasons for Shirley's popularity, Hollywood was grateful to her for what she had already done for the movie business. On February 27, 1935, she was the first child actor ever to receive an Academy Award. It was presented to Shirley not for any single performance but "in grateful recognition of her outstanding contribution to screen entertainment

during the year 1934." The traditional Oscar statue was scaled down to child size just for her.

Shirley knew she was going to receive the award. She also knew it was supposed to be a surprise. All evening she asked anybody who would listen, "When are they going to surprise me?" When the time came, she played her part and acted surprised. It was all like a game to her.

In that same year, Fox and another film studio called 20th Century agreed to merge and become 20th Century Fox. There was a special dinner in the grand ballroom of a Beverly Hills hotel to celebrate the union of the two studios. Shirley attended with her parents.

Sam Hellman, a screenwriter who worked for Fox, saw Shirley. He reached down and scooped her up and lifted her high over his head. Suddenly, a terrible silence fell over the ballroom. Hellman later said, "I realized then what I was doing. Here I was holding practically all the assets of 20th Century Fox in my hands. It scared me so I nearly dropped her." Little Shirley didn't understand what had happened. She was used to being celebrated. She did not realize that the studio people loved the money she made for them more than they loved her.

But she was a star, and she knew it. Once, when a reporter was interviewing Gertrude Temple, Shirley piped up and said, "Why don't you interview me? I'm the star."

But as time went on, she grew bored. The reporters always seemed to ask her the same questions. She didn't have much patience with photographers, either. One time a photographer took too long setting up his camera. Little Shirley warned him, "Make the pictures now or not at all. I can't wait for you."

Years later, after she was grown up, Shirley told a Hollywood reporter, "I was really something in those days, wasn't I? I don't know why anybody tolerated me. I had an ego. But they helped it along."

3

Little Big Shot

The studio executives helped Shirley's ego along a lot. All the while, they were mostly interested in the money she could make for them. Her health was a serious matter. Whenever she caught a cold, the studio sent her down to Palm Springs to get well. And when she lost a tooth, it was a major crisis.

The studio built a special little house for her, with a child-sized bathroom, a complete kitchen, a bedroom for taking naps, and a large living room. Out back was a small yard with chickens and rabbits for her to play with. There was also a special trailer that

was pulled up next to the indoor stage on the studio lot where she was working and that she stayed in when filming was done "on location" off the studio lot.

All this was very nice, but things like special houses and trailers also kept Shirley isolated from the other people on the set. Stagehands were given strict orders not to play with her. The studio executives did not want her to come into contact with other people on the set. She might get hurt, she might be bothered.

She wasn't even allowed to play with child costars. In *Bright Eyes*, one of the 1934 Fox films, Shirley starred with Jane Withers, another child actress. Withers later said that she worried about Shirley because she didn't think that Shirley was having a very good time. Young Jane really wanted to get to know Shirley, but the assistant director told her mother that Jane couldn't play with Shirley or even talk with her except when they were in a scene together.

Another of her young costars, Delmar Watson, remembered playing horseshoes with her for exactly two minutes. Then Shirley's bodyguard found her and told her she wasn't supposed to be away from the trailer. Shirley did not argue; she went with the man. Watson also remembers thinking that Shirley must have been very lonely.

Shirley herself has never complained about being lonely or feeling isolated during those years. She may have realized that her stardom was very important to her mother.

Gertrude Temple was always there, doing Shirley's hair, reading her scripts to her, calling out, "Sparkle, Shirley, sparkle." Even when she was very young, Shirley probably realized that the money she was bringing in was important to the family.

For Shirley, acting in movies was fun, kind of like a game. But it was a game in which you came prepared and did not make mistakes. She not only learned her own lines, but those of her costars as well. She even corrected her costars. At one point during the filming of *Stand Up and Cheer*, a movie she made with actor James Dunn in 1934, Dunn fluffed a line. Little Shirley stopped and scolded him, telling him what he should have said and done. The producers and director thought it was so funny that they kept that conversation between the tiny star and the big star in the movie.

Around the studio, she'd gotten the nickname "One-take Shirley" because she could do a conversation, song, or dance in the first filmed try.

She had, finally, started school. She did not attend regular school classes with other children. Instead, she had a special tutor named Miss Klampt. Shirley called her "Klammie." For three hours a day, Miss Klampt taught Shirley spelling and geography and arithmetic and all the other subjects that Shirley would have learned in a regular classroom. Miss Klampt also gave Shirley tests to make sure she was learning her lessons. Sometimes, Miss Klampt felt that Shirley was doing too much movie work and not enough schoolwork. She wasn't afraid to tell the director to stop shooting and let Shirley pay attention to her studies. Shirley usually did what she was told.

Shirley always played a good little girl in her films, but she was never sickly-sweet. Her cuteness was real and unaffected. In all her films, Shirley manages to find people who love her and who will take care of her. She also helps turn a lot of grown-ups from selfish people into loving people. Always, things turn out happily in the end.

Not long after Fox Films put her under contract, the Temples bought a new house. But it was right on the street, and fans kept driving by and peering in the windows. So the Temples built a big house surrounded by several acres of land.

The house was large and comfortable, with a twelve-foot fence around it. There was a swimming pool and a badminton court. Just for Shirley there was an electrically-powered merry-go-round and a stable with two ponies. There was also a "playhouse" which was large enough for a whole family. It had a huge main room with a movie screen and a soda fountain and a big fireplace. Later, a bowling alley was built in the basement. Thanks to the money she earned making movies, her family was rich.

The only thing lacking was playmates for Shirley. Her brothers were teenagers who thought it was very nice that their little sister was a star, but they didn't have much time for her. Gertrude Temple would sometimes invite a neighbor's child over to play with Shirley. Otherwise, her only regular friend was Mary Lou Islieb, the little girl who was her movie stand-in,

she was such a big star. She, too, had to be content with all the toys money could buy because she was not allowed to be an ordinary kid.

She was a very bright child. She came to understand early on that in her small world one of the most important things, besides being cute, was being a good actress. She was getting better and better at it. When Shirley was younger, her directors had to play tricks on her to get her to cry. One trick that worked well was to tell her that she could not have any lunch. She would begin to wail, and the director would tell the cameras to roll. But later, after she understood better what was expected of her, a director only had to say, "Shirley, think of the saddest thing you can," and the tears would come for the cameras.

The more movies she did, the more professional she became. But she could also be a pain in the neck, especially when there were other children in the film. Shirley decided, with some reason, that she knew better than any other child actor how to behave on a set. But sometimes she was too bossy.

In 1936, Shirley starred in the 20th Century Fox film *Heidi*. There were a lot of other children in the film, and Shirley decided to take charge of them. Every time she heard a direction, she turned and gave it to one of the kids.

The director, Allan Dwan, watched Shirley for a

while. He decided that she was lonely and didn't really know how to get along with the other children. He saw that she was kept away from them and had grown used to being "the star."

He knew that Shirley needed attention. He also realized that if he was going to make the movie he needed to give her that attention. He had little badges made up with SHIRLEY TEMPLE POLICE stamped on them and said that every child on the set had to join the force and obey Shirley.

"It began to backfire a little," Dwan said many years later. "Shirley took it so seriously she said no child who was not a member of the corps could work in a picture . . . so we signed up every kid we hired. She was a little big shot and loved it."

4

Not So Cute
Anymore

In a number of her films, Shirley was paired with a black character. The helpless little girl and the equally helpless black managed to succeed together. She made three films with the actor Stepin Fetchit, whose real name was Lincoln Perry, and one with the actress Hattie McDaniel. Blacks appeared so often in her films, in fact, that there was a joke in the movie industry that a Temple picture was not complete without at least one black.

Her favorite black costar was Bill "Bojangles" Robinson. She first starred with him in *The Little Colonel* in 1935. They appeared together in *The Littlest Rebel* that same year, and in *Rebecca of Sunnybrook Farm* in 1938. Bojangles and Shirley Temple were a popular combination. The films they did together remain among the most popular Shirley Temple films.

Robinson was almost sixty years old by the time he became Shirley Temple's most beloved costar. He'd already had a long career as a tap dancer.

Robinson's most famous routine was the stair dance, in which he tapped up and down a staircase. As soon as he was signed to do *The Little Colonel*, the scriptwriters wrote a stair dance into the script. Robinson played a servant in the big Southern mansion who danced to make little Shirley happy. Bill realized that while he might be able to tap up and down the big staircase of the mansion, seven-year-old Shirley could not. So, he taught her to get the extra tap per step that was so important to the routine. He told her to kick the front of each step with her toe. It took him a while to make her understand it all, but once she got it, she performed beautifully. Overjoyed, Robinson bent down and kissed her feet, saying, "Uncle Bill doesn't tell her feet where to go. Her heart tells her." Their stair dance was the highlight of the film.

The two became very close. Bill Robinson started carrying around more than 15 photos of Shirley. She called him Uncle Billy and wanted to be with him all the time on the set.

During the shooting of *The Little Colonel*, Shirley caught a cold. As usual, the studio sent her down to the Desert Inn in Palm Springs to get better. Since Shirley was in the middle of learning the stair dance, Robinson went to Palm Springs, too, so they could continue practicing.

Shirley was delighted that Uncle Billy was there. She wanted to know where he was staying at the Desert Inn. He told her he was staying in the drivers' quarters, which was the only place a black was allowed to stay at the Desert Inn, no matter how famous he was. "But why aren't you staying in a cottage?" Shirley wanted to know.

"Don't you worry, honey," said Robinson, "I'm staying with *my* chauffeur."

Shirley realized that it was pretty dumb to make Bill stay with servants just because he was black.

In 1938, Shirley starred with Robinson in *The Littlest Rebel*. Once again, Robinson played a family servant, but this time he had a more responsible role. The Yankees invade Shirley's mansion home during her birthday party, and take her father prisoner. She and Uncle Billy make money by dancing. They go to Washington, D.C. and ask President Lincoln to pardon her father. This was the first time in a Hollywood movie that a black character was made responsible for a white life. Shirley didn't understand the importance of that at the time, but later she was very proud of it.

A friend of Robinson's named Rae Samuels Forkins remembered how well Bill and Shirley worked together. One day, when Shirley made a mistake, "Bill stopped the rehearsal. He said, 'Why don't you let that child alone? She's hungry and she's tired.' He said to her, 'Come on, Shirley,' and they went over for a rest."

Forkins continues, "She was getting a little chubby by then, and she wasn't allowed to eat ice cream. She and Bill used to love to eat ice cream together, but now he had to eat it by himself . . . They had about a 15-minute rest and Bill's quart of ice cream was brought to him. He got busy eating the ice cream and, when nobody was looking, he handed it down to her."

By that time, Shirley was indeed getting chubby, and all those ringlets no longer seemed to fit her round, maturing face. By 1939 she had slid down to Number 5 on the box office lists. One newspaper writer, using a word that means she had been doing the same thing for too many years and ought to retire, called her a "superannuated sunbeam."

20th Century Fox didn't have many roles for her anymore, for she was too old to play a child and too young to play a teenager. On the other hand, they didn't want to "loan her out" to other studios. They refused to loan her to Metro-Goldwyn-Mayer to play Dorothy in *The Wizard of Oz*, so Judy Garland got the part. Shirley Temple's later film career might have been very different if she had gotten that role.

The Temples decided it was time for Shirley to stop concentrating on movies and start getting an education in a real school. They ended her exclusive contract with 20th Century Fox in May 1940. The studio gave Shirley a few of her old costumes and her rehearsal piano. There was no big farewell party for the young "has-been."

In the fall of 1940, she enrolled at Westlake School for Girls, a private, exclusive school near Beverly Hills. She had a hard time there for the first few weeks, because the other girls thought she would be stuck up. She said later, "That first week, one of the students . . . startled me by inviting every girl in the group to a party except me. I was not hurt, just surprised—surprised to learn that being Shirley Temple didn't solve everything." Shirley made a point of not acting like a star, and after a while the other girls came to accept her.

From time to time, she still did movies for 20th Century Fox, MGM, and United Artists. In February 1941 she signed a 40-week contract with MGM. Because she was still so young, she had to have her contract approved in court. The judge asked her if

she really wanted to return to work. "Oh my, yes," said Shirley. "School is so dull." She still got a great deal of fan mail. But she was no longer "America's Sweetheart" or a star in Hollywood.

As a teenager, Shirley didn't have much luck getting more roles. She was not pretty enough to attract movie audiences. Young female stars like Elizabeth Taylor were great beauties and were getting the important roles.

Shirley also suffered from having such an innocent image in the eyes of the public. People could not accept her growing up and playing romantic roles. In 1947 she costarred in *That Hagen Girl* with a young actor named Ronald Reagan. In the movie the two fall in love. The Reagan character even says, "I love you" to the Shirley character. But in previews, the audience didn't like that at all, and so the scene was taken out of the film. America did not want Little Shirley Temple to grow up.

5

Facing the Real World

By this time, the United States had entered World War II, and Shirley appeared in United Service Organization (USO) entertainment shows, visited wounded soldiers, and did whatever else she could to help the war effort. One young soldier was facing an operation to remove his leg. He asked her to stay with him during the operation, and she agreed. She later explained, "If he could stand having it off, I could stand helping him."

During the war years, she began dating a sergeant in the Army named John Agar. They became engaged

in April 1945, two weeks before her seventeenth birthday. The engagement put Shirley back on the front pages of newspapers—America could not believe that Little Shirley Temple was old enough to be engaged.

Shirley graduated from Westlake that June. Three months later, she and John Agar were married. When they had gotten engaged, she had told her mother that they would wait a couple of years before they got married. But in the summer of 1945 she was worried that John might be sent to fight overseas, and she changed her mind. Much later, looking back, Shirley realized that she had also rushed to marry John because she wanted to be the one who got married first of the girls in her class at Westlake. "I wanted to win the race," she explained. "This is a dangerous basis for a marriage."

The newlyweds moved into the "playhouse" on the Temple property. The movie screen and soda fountain were removed to make a proper living room and dining room. Shirley took cooking classes and tried to play the role of housewife. But when another movie offer came along, she hired a housekeeper.

Meanwhile, the American public could not get enough of Shirley Temple and her young husband. They appeared in two RKO films together. Shirley became pregnant during the filming of *Fort Apache*, and was overjoyed. But the people at RKO were not; they were convinced that the American public did not want Little Shirley Temple to be a mother.

Whatever the public wanted, a baby was on the way. Linda Susan was born January 29, 1948, three months before Shirley's twentieth birthday. Bill Robinson sent the baby a white rabbit coat. Shirley was delighted with her new baby, but by this time she did not feel close enough to her husband to share her joy with him. They had gotten married too young, and the marriage wasn't working out.

Shirley told a Hollywood reporter, "John is a nice boy, but he's a little mixed up." By the fall of 1949, Shirley had filed for divorce. At the end of the year, she had also appeared in her last feature film, *A Kiss for Corliss*, for Warner Brothers.

For Shirley, it was hard enough to accept the idea that her marriage had failed. It was also hard for her to deal with the feeling that she had failed a lot of other young girls. So many girls had written to her about their own wish to marry young and about their trouble with their parents over that. She felt as if she had let them down. "One of the mistakes I made was always acting the happy wife in public," she said later. "I felt the responsibility of being Shirley Temple."

Shirley had to face the fact that life wasn't all happy endings, like in the movies. She also realized that it was time for her to have a private life, a life of her own. She decided that she could not try to be America's Sweetheart anymore. She had to be an independent adult. She did not move back in with her parents, but stayed in her own house with Susan. She would not talk to reporters.

When her parents suggested that it would be a nice change for her if they all took a vacation in Hawaii, she was eager to go. She had visited Hawaii three times as a child, and all her memories of that place were happy ones.

There were even more happy memories in store, for during that vacation in Hawaii Shirley met Charles Black. He was assistant to the president of the Hawaii Pineapple Company. He had been born and raised in San Francisco, had served in the Navy during World War II, and had never seen a Shirley Temple movie!

Charles Black was not even interested in meeting Shirley Temple. The first time he was invited to a reception for her, he went surfing instead! But a few days later, they met at another party. Before the evening was over, he asked her out to dinner. It was love at first sight. Says Shirley, "It's corny, but it's all true. You know, some enchanted evening across a crowded room."

On December 15, 1951, less than two weeks after Shirley's divorce from John Agar became final, she and Charles Black were secretly married in Monterey, California.

They kept the marriage secret because they didn't want reporters and photographers all over the place. And Shirley, now Mrs. Charles Black, wanted to have a private life. As her husband changed jobs, she moved with him to different parts of the country. Not long after their marriage, the Korean conflict broke out. Charles Black was called back to Navy duty at the Pentagon in Washington, D.C. During that time, Charles, Jr., and Lori were born.

When Charles, Jr., was six months old, Shirley refused to have him christened at her local church. She wanted a private ceremony, but the pastor wanted a big christening "event." Shirley objected, and the pastor told her that she would always "belong to the public." But Shirley said that didn't mean her baby did. She had Charles, and later Lori, christened at home.

They lived in Bethesda, Maryland, and the neighbors were not used to having a movie star around. They couldn't believe that Shirley did her own shopping at the local supermarket and even mowed her own lawn. One time Shirley was driving the lawn mower on her property. A man in a car out on the street called to her to get out of the way so he could take a picture of "Shirley Temple's house"!

In 1953, Charles got a job in San Francisco. Shirley still did her own shopping and cooking and house-keeping, and she still fiercely guarded her family life from the prying eyes of the public. Once, when Susan was in a school play, a newspaper reported it. Shirley became so angry that she took Susan out of the school. "My only desire," she said, "is to be retired and left alone."

Although she guarded her family's privacy closely, Shirley didn't spend all her time at home. She did a great deal of volunteer work during the years when her children were growing up. She volunteered at a clinic for emotionally disturbed children and at Stanford University Medical Center in Palo Alto.

Her special charity was the Multiple Sclerosis Foundation. That disease affects the nervous system and can cripple its victims. In 1950, when Shirley was thirty, her older brother, George, learned that he had the disease. After a while, he had to use a wheelchair and could walk only with two aluminum canes. Shirley found the best way to deal with her own grief. She went to work for the group that was trying to find a way to fight the disease.

From time to time, she also appeared on television. In early 1958, not long before her thirtieth birthday, she began filming a series called "The Shirley Temple Storybook." The stories were classic fairy tales like

"Beauty and the Beast" and "Mother Goose." Shirley acted in a few of them, but more often she was just the narrator.

This was a family decision. She had asked her husband and children how they felt about her being away in Los Angeles to film the series. They had said they wouldn't mind her being away sometimes, but not a lot. So, rather than act in many of the shows, which would have kept her away a lot, she narrated many of them. She could do the narrations for several shows in a single recording session. Shirley's children were so excited about her being in the "Shirley Temple Storybook" series that they all decided they wanted to appear in the stories. All three appeared in "Mother Goose," and all three decided that being actors wasn't very exciting. Charles didn't like having to wear makeup and sit around waiting for his scenes. Lori complained that her costume was "old-fashioned." Susan enjoyed the experience but decided she would rather write stories than act in them. That was the end of the acting careers of the three children of Shirley Temple.

6

Shirley on the World Stage

In 1967, Shirley decided to become another kind of public figure. She wanted to run for Congress. Ever since Charles had worked at the Pentagon in Washington, D.C., Shirley had been very interested in politics and public affairs. At the time, a Republican president, Dwight D. Eisenhower, was in the White House. Shirley was a strong believer in the Republican party.

By 1967, Shirley's children were old enough not to need her at home all the time. She had a real desire to make a contribution to public life. She decided to run for a seat in Congress.

Her whole family agreed to help her. Charles was her campaign manager. The children licked stamps and sealed envelopes. Everyone was with her when she announced her candidacy at the end of August.

In her speech that day, Shirley said she was against the war in Vietnam. She promised that she would do all she could to get the United States out of it. "It is not progress for the largest military power in the world to be . . . in an apparently endless war with one of the smallest and weakest countries in the world," she said.

She was also against high taxes. She was for stronger laws against drug use and child pornography (the use of children in sexual or violent magazines and films). Grown-up Shirley Temple Black would have fought against the kinds of films Little Shirley Temple had appeared in at the age of four.

Being Shirley Temple Black, former child star, helped her in some ways. Most people recognized her name right away, and name recognition is very important in politics. Of course, many people were dismayed that she could be old enough to run for Congress, for if she was that old, then they must be even older!

On the other hand, being a former child star worked against her because it was hard to make people take her seriously. After a while, she grew tired of hearing "On the Good Ship Lollipop" every time she made an appearance at a political event. Once, getting mad, she reminded a reporter, "Little Shirley Temple is not running."

In the election, which was held on November 14, 1967, she lost. But the loss didn't get Shirley down. "I plan to dedicate my life and energies to public service," she said, "because I think my country needs it now more than ever."

Soon she was working to get Richard M. Nixon, a Republican, elected president in the 1968 election. She went to 22 states and 46 cities and was the star attraction at rallies for Nixon. She also went to several cities in Europe to urge Americans living there to vote in the election back home by absentee ballot.

Richard Nixon won the election as president in November 1968. He formally took office in January 1969.

The following summer, Shirley was named to the United States delegation to the United Nations. This was a thank-you from the president for her help in his campaign. It also followed a tradition. In the past, other popular figures in the entertainment world had been what are called "public" members of the U.N.

Some people complained about her lack of experience. But one delegate said, "So what! If she's been serious about her work in American health groups, if she cares about people—in her own country and oth-

ers—if she's warm and friendly with the other delegates—she's a diplomat."

Shirley wanted the world to know that she was going to take her job seriously. She was assigned to committees on the environment, youth, refugees, and the peaceful uses of outer space. She read all she could on these subjects and faithfully attended meetings.

She also became interested in Africa. "I became convinced that our country was not giving enough attention to Africa and Latin America. I made a vow to myself . . . to see where we could mutually benefit each other. Because of this, I wanted to serve somewhere in black Africa."

One day in 1969, she attended a meeting at the White House with Secretary of State Henry Kissinger. Shirley asked Dr. Kissinger what his feelings were on Namibia. Kissinger looked puzzled. He didn't recognize the name. He knew it as South West Africa, which the white people of South Africa took over. Shirley recalled later, "I went over to the map and pointed it out. I also told him that Namibia was a raging topic at the U.N."

In 1971, U.N. delegates invited Shirley to visit Egypt. She expected to have tea with Jihan Sadat, wife of the president of Egypt. She did not expect to meet the president himself.

When President Anwar el-Sadat himself appeared,

Shirley was so surprised that she stood up without remembering that she had her purse in her lap. Everything in it spilled onto the floor! The president helped her pick it all up. Then he told her that he had loved the movie *Heidi*. In fact, he wanted a copy of it. Shirley said she would send him one, and later she did.

Then President Sadat gave her a secret message for President Nixon. "Tell your president, I am the first Arab leader to truly want peace," he said. He meant that he wanted to make peace with Israel, and Shirley was excited. The problem between Israel and its Arab neighbors was one of the biggest problems in the world. But President Nixon never followed up on the "secret" offer of peace that Shirley brought back. Not until eight years later did President Jimmy Carter, a Democrat, get President Sadat of Egypt and Prime Minister Begin of Israel together to talk peace.

As 1971 ended, President Nixon appointed Shirley special assistant to the chairman of the President's Council on Environmental Quality.

Then one day she found a lump in her breast. She telephoned her doctor and went for an examination, and learned that it was cancer. Shirley had to have an operation. It was hard for her, but she did not spend a lot of time feeling sorry for herself. Instead, she realized that she was in a special position to help other women.

Shirley Temple Black was the first well-known woman to talk openly about her operation. She had a bedside news conference. "The only reason I am telling this," she said, "is because I fervently hope other women will not be afraid to go to their doctors when they note any unusual symptoms. There is almost certain cure for this form of cancer if caught early enough." After that press conference, the hospital was flooded with mail for Shirley.

Shirley soon resumed her duties for the government. She was in Caracas, Venezuela, in August 1974, when she learned that Republican President Gerald R. Ford had appointed her United States Ambassador to Ghana. She talked it over with her husband and children, then she accepted.

Most U.S. ambassadors are people who have been in government for a long time. Rarely does a former movie star get to be an ambassador. Some people said that the appointment was a political payoff. But Shirley and her husband had never given a lot of money to the Republican Party.

Secretary of State Henry Kissinger told her that she was chosen partly because of their conversation back in 1969. She had impressed him with her questions about Namibia.

Shirley wanted to be the best U.S. ambassador to Ghana that she could be. She read everything she could about that African country. She went to more than 50 meetings. There, people from the U.S. State Department explained the history and culture and politics of Africa.

Ghana is on the west coast of Africa. Thirty-five American companies had offices or factories in Ghana, and the two countries had good trade relations. The United States wanted to increase trade. One reason that a woman was chosen as U.S. Ambassador to Ghana may have been that women are very important in their society. Families are traced through the female line, and women are very active in business in Ghana. Many Ghanaian women were proud to see a woman ambassador from America.

Shirley moved into the ambassador's house in Accra, the nation's capital, in December 1974. Charles was working in food development projects. He and her daughter, Susan, moved in with her. Susan wrote magazine articles about life in Ghana. The two younger children remained in school in California. They visited on holidays and vacations.

One of the first things Shirley did was to go out and meet people. She called on government leaders and American businessmen. But she also visited markets and other places where she knew she would find ordinary people. She learned at least a few words in each of the major languages, Fanti, Gwa, and Ti. She

did not pretend she was better than anyone else. Once she even shocked some visiting Americans by welcoming them to the ambassador's house wearing a robe and running shoes, while chewing gum.

Shirley was very popular among the Ghanaians. Soon, newborn babies, boys as well as girls, were being named in her honor. An example: Kofi Shirley Temple Black Issifu. Shirley was also the first ambassador ever invited to speak before the Market Women's Association in Accra.

While in Ghana, Ambassador Black also did her part to improve U.S. relations with other nations. Her daughter Susan wrote that, during one afternoon party, Shirley played Ping-Pong with the ambassador from the People's Republic of China. Not long afterward, Susan reported, "The Chinese Ambassador paid a courtesy call (a private, friendly visit) on Mom at her office." This had never been done before.

Sometimes Shirley found that being an ambassador was difficult. Sometimes there were demonstrations against U.S. policies outside the official U.S. government building in Accra. But most of the time she found the job very enjoyable.

In 1976, President Ford appointed her Chief of Protocol (proper manners and relations) for the White House in Washington, D.C. Shirley didn't want to leave Africa. But she believed that she should do whatever her president asked. Also, she liked the idea of being the first woman Chief of Protocol in American history.

The Ghanaians were sorry to see her go. So was the U.S. State Department. Many of its members had been against Shirley. Now they admitted that she had been one of the best ambassadors ever.

Shirley and Charles took an apartment in Washington. Charles moved the headquarters of his business there. Shirley set about learning to be chief of protocol. Her job was to help visiting diplomats and presidents, to plan the seating at banquets, to make sure people joined a reception line in the proper order, and to manage other details of diplomatic good manners. The job involved going to a lot of parties. Shirley had never liked parties, but mostly she enjoyed her work.

She was not on the job long. In the national election of November 1976, Democrat Jimmy Carter beat Republican President Gerald Ford. A job like Chief of Protocol is an appointed job, just like being an ambassador. A new Democratic president wanted to choose his own people for those jobs.

Shirley and Charles returned to California and Shirley went back to private life. She had her volunteer activities. A few years later, she became a grandmother. Susan had married a man she had met while in Ghana. Little Teresa was born on December 20, 1980. Shirley said Teresa was the best Christmas gift ever.

From time to time, Shirley has been called back to Washington to talk to new diplomats about what to expect in other countries. She has also made no secret of her interest in another ambassador's post in Africa.

In September 1986 she commented on the problem of apartheid (say it, "apart-hate") in South Africa. This system gives blacks and other people of color few rights. They are the majority of people in that country, but they cannot even vote. The whites control the government, which tells nonwhites where they may live and work and what they can learn in school. Shirley said she would like a job as "apartheid-busting ambassador to South Africa . . . I like to solve problems," she explained, "and that's one of the biggest ones we've got in the world right now."

Shirley also works hard for the Republican party. She continues to be in great demand to speak at political events. She knows that the name "Shirley Temple" still has a kind of magic for many people. But she also realizes that "Little Shirley opens up doors for Shirley Temple Black. (But) if big Shirley can't produce, the doors close."

She feels that she *has* produced. She has spent much of her adult life trying to make a real contribution to the world. She accepts the idea that as a cute child movie star she brightened the lives of many people during the Depression. But she is more interested in talking about what she has done since she was old enough to make real choices for herself. She is proud of her long and happy marriage to Charles Black, her children, and her work for the government.

One time Shirley Temple Black was asked how she wanted to be remembered. She said only that she hoped "people will remember that I *lived*, that I didn't just exist."

ABOUT THIS BOOK

I was not yet born when Shirley Temple was the darling of Hollywood. But I remember watching reruns of her movies on television when I was young, and rooting for her to triumph over hard times. I became interested in her as a person when I was writing a biography of Bill "Bo-jangles" Robinson. Like Robinson, Little Shirley Temple had a big heart. As I read and learned more about the grown-up Shirley Temple Black, I realized that she took that part of her, along with her dimples, into adulthood.

Shirley Temple published an autobiography, *My Young Life*, in 1945 when she was 17. She has not written about herself since then.

In 1986, I met Shirley Temple Black in person. We were both members of the Statue of Liberty Bicentennial Commission. She was very reserved and quiet, but when she smiled some of the dimpled sparkle of Little Shirley Temple came through. I wondered how it must be for someone to be famous practically all her life. But it would not have been polite to ask her.

Shirley Temple Black wants to be known for the life she has lived as a grown-up. It is interesting to learn about how "Big Shirley" has been able to establish an identity separate from that of Little Shirley Temple, child star.

JH.